WITHDRAWN

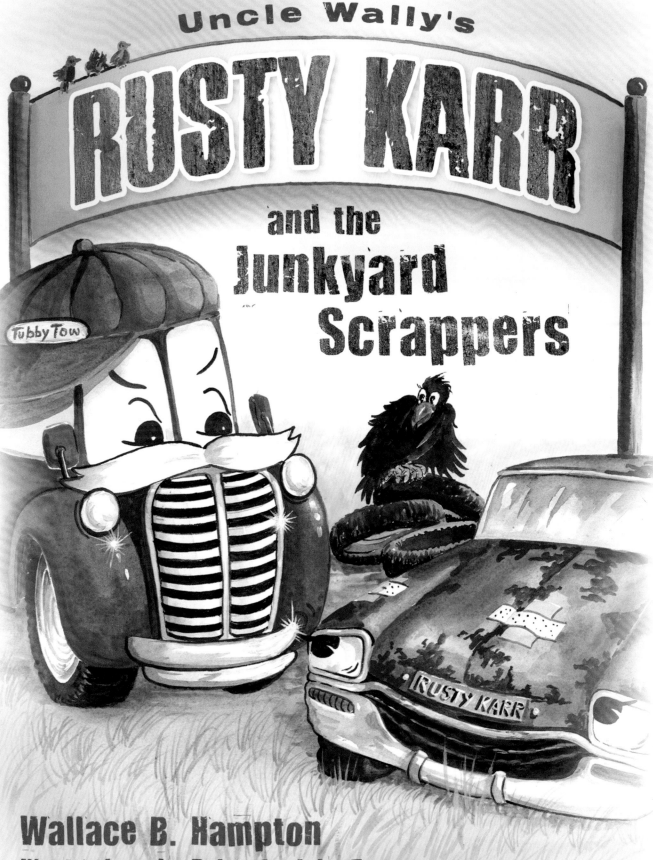

Uncle Wally's
RUSTY KARR
and the
Junkyard
Scrappers

Wallace B. Hampton
Illustrations by Doina Cociuba Terrano

Book Publishers Network
P. O. Box 2256
Bothell, WA 98041
425-483-3040

10 9 8 7 6 5 4 3 2 1

ISBN 13: 978-1-937454-94-4

Rusty Karr and the
junkyard scrappers became
good friends one day.

Rusty was in a parking lot
when Tubby Tow Truck
took him away.

A hook went under his bumper and
raised him way up high.

Tears rolled out of his headlights.
Poor Rusty started to cry.

Rusty had a couple of scratches,
dents and other stuff.

That is why the tow truck made
a mistake and towed poor
Rusty off.

Rusty Karr tugged and pulled, but his
strength was no match.

Every time Rusty would tug and pull,
he would get another scratch.

Rusty Karr tugged and pulled so much
his bumper got very sore.
Rusty ran out of energy. He couldn't
tug and pull any more.

Tubby pulled into a car-
scrap yard and dropped
off poor old Rusty.

There were so many broken-down
cars, and the air was very musty.

There were cars that were
really broken and some that
weren't so bad.

Being there was the end of the line,
and that made Rusty sad.

Two men came up to Rusty.
They had the scent of oil
and must.

One man said to the other one,
"This car can be crushed."

Rusty Karr had no energy and thought that he was through.

Then something magical happened.
Rusty Karr became brand new.

What really happened
wasn't magic at all.
The cars all gathered
together, medium,
big, and small.

They were all different in every
way. One even had a hole.
But even though they're different,
they had a common goal.

They talked about their problem that all the scrappers share.

Rusty Karr
realized that the
junkyard
scrappers care.

So they worked
together very hard.
Parts were flying
all around.

They put each other
together and didn't even
make a sound.

The two men came and saw the cars.
Their jaws dropped to the ground.

Dedication

I proudly dedicate this book to my nieces and nephews.
You make me proud to be Uncle Wally.

Acknowledgements

Tucker Kerr and Phil Connolly, I would like to give you a special thanks for guiding me on the right path of the beginning of an amazing journey of books.

Thanks you so much: James S. Westall and his 1940 Ford Coupe aka Speedy; Rex Rich and his 1965 Ford Fairlane 500 aka Flip; Mitch Halgren and his 1955 Pontiac Sedan aka Zoomy; Ed Hervey and his 1958 Edsel aka Classy; Patti Hampton and her old photographs that show an old tow truck aka Tubby Tow; Melvin and David Jenkins and their 1955 Cadillac aka Flashy; Gary Shields and his 1941 two door Ford Sedan aka Tinker and his 1956 Ford Customline two door hard top aka Revy; George Weimer and his 1956 F 100 aka Tucker; and to the guy who allowed me to take pictures of his 1958 Oldsmobile aka Rusty Karr. I am forever grateful—they are the perfect cars.

And to Patti Hampton, Earl Kingsley, and Tucker Kerr for allowing me to use your names in the store fronts and to Tammie Fidecaro and countless others whose enthusiastic energy has been a great driving force to keep me going.

Watch for Uncle Wally's next books:

Rusty Karr and the Junkyard Scrappers – On the Run

My Lost Teddy Bear